TOMORROW ON ROCKY POND

by Lynn Reiser

GREENWILLOW BOOKS   New York

Watercolor paints and a black pen were used for the full-color art.
The text type is Century Old Style.

Printed in Singapore by Tien Wah Press
First Edition 10 9 8 7 6 5 4 3 2 1

Library of Congress Cataloging-in-Publication Data
Reiser, Lynn.
Tomorrow on Rocky Pond/by Lynn Reiser.
     p.   cm.
Summary: Vacationing in the country, a child anticipates
tomorrow's activities, from fishing in Rocky Pond to
walking in the woods and observing animals.
ISBN 0-688-10672-2. ISBN 0-688-10673-0 (lib. bdg.)
[1. Ponds—Fiction.   2. Fishing—Fiction.
3. Animals—Fiction.]   I. Title.
PZ7.R27745To   1993   [E]—dc20   91-45801   CIP   AC

To yesterdays
and tomorrows
on rocky ponds—

Today we drove and drove.
Then we unpacked.
Now it is time to hurry to bed

because tomorrow
we are going fishing on Rocky Pond.

Tomorrow we will wake up
and there will be mist on the lake
and sparkles on the spider webs

and the loons
will be calling

and we will have
blueberry pancakes
and blueberry muffins
and blueberries with cream
for breakfast.

And then we will put on our fishing clothes–
we will put on
our chamois shirts
and our blue jeans
and our fishing vests
and our canoe shoes
and our sun screen
and our bug spray
and our fishing hats
and our sunglasses
and our knapsacks
and we will pull our socks
over our blue jeans.

And we will remember to bring
the
berry
basket

and
the thermos

and
the picnic

and
the life vests

and
the
float
cushions

and the
bathing
suits

and
the paddles

and the
fly box

and
the fishing
net

and
the fishing
rods

and the fishing creel

and
the flashlights.

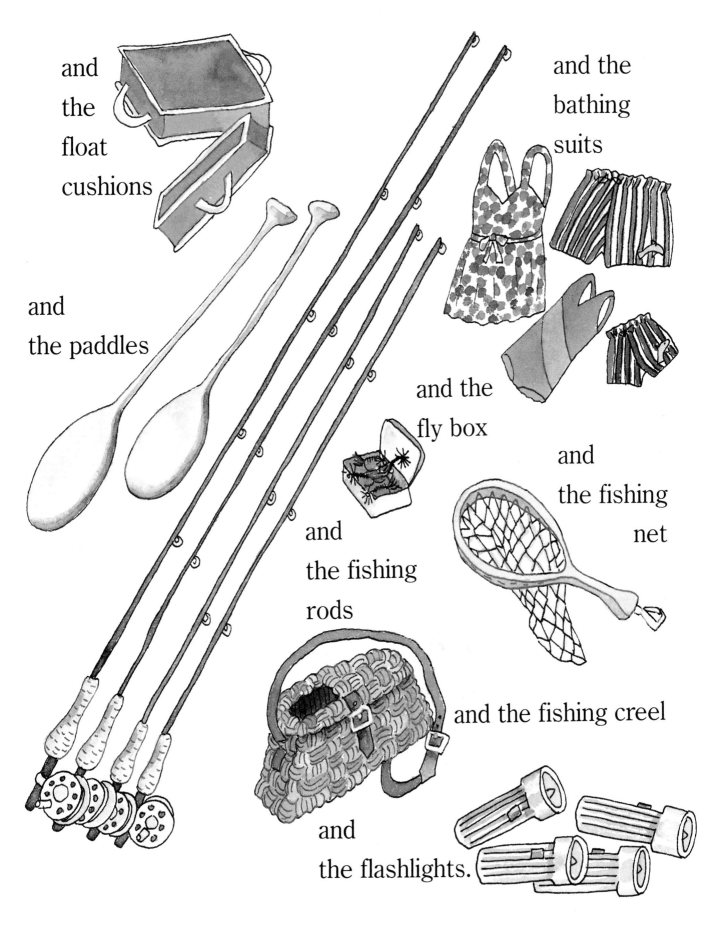

Then we will walk through the woods
and we will hear
the cicadas and the woodpecker
and see the rocks and the moss

and the mushrooms

and the white birch trees with the bark peeling

and the big gray trees

and the little gray trees—

and maybe we will see
the deer watching us.

We will pick
a lot of raspberries
and eat
some raspberries—
and maybe
we will
surprise
a family
of snowshoe
rabbits.
(But we only
call them
rabbits.
They are really
hares.)

And then we will have a drink from our thermos.

And we will keep walking
and walking
until we come to our canoe
waiting in a tree
beside Rocky Pond.

And we will take down the canoe
and slide it into the water
and little frogs will jump into the water too.

Then we will put on our life vests
and paddle across by the beaver lodge—
but the beavers will be asleep.

And we will land on a flat rock
and have a picnic lunch
and we will have lemonade
and peanut butter sandwiches
and chocolate chip cookies
and pickles

and
the Canada jays
and the chipmunks
will have peanut butter sandwiches
and chocolate chip cookies too—but not pickles.

By then we will feel very sleepy
and we will take a nap on the soft moss.

And then, tomorrow on Rocky Pond,
we will put on our bathing suits
and have a swim

and the tadpoles
and the minnows
will tickle our toes.

And we will put our clothes back on
and pick up all the trash
and get back into the canoe
and now it will be time for fishing.

The kingfisher will be fishing too
and the great blue heron will be fishing too
and the merganser ducks will be fishing too.

And the loons
will be fishing too

and sometimes
the mother loon
will give the baby loon
a fish

and sometimes
the father loon
will give the baby loon
a fish.

And sometimes
a dragonfly
will sit on the line

and sometimes
a water strider
will skate by

and when the trout fly lands
it will look like a mayfly landing.

And maybe while we are fishing
we will paddle close to a big rock

and maybe
the rock will
stand up–

WHOOSH–

and maybe
the rock
will be
a moose.

And if it is,
we will paddle away very fast—
so fast
that maybe we will not notice
that there is a big fish
caught on the line.

And if there is,
we will catch the fish
in the net

and put it in the creel
with ferns to keep it cool.

By then it will be starting to get dark
and it will be time to come home.
The beavers will be waking up–
and maybe one will slap its tail.

And the loons will be calling

and we will paddle back across Rocky Pond

and put the canoe
back in the tree

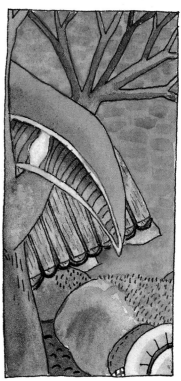

and walk home through the woods
with the fireflies.
And the woods will be dark

and we will shine our flashlights–

and maybe we will see an owl watching us.

And finally we will be home again.

We will have trout for dinner
and raspberry pie for dessert

and then we will sit
on the porch

and watch the stars come out
and the moon come up

and listen to the loons calling.

But now it is time to hurry to sleep
because tomorrow
we are going fishing on Rocky Pond–

and tomorrow is almost here.

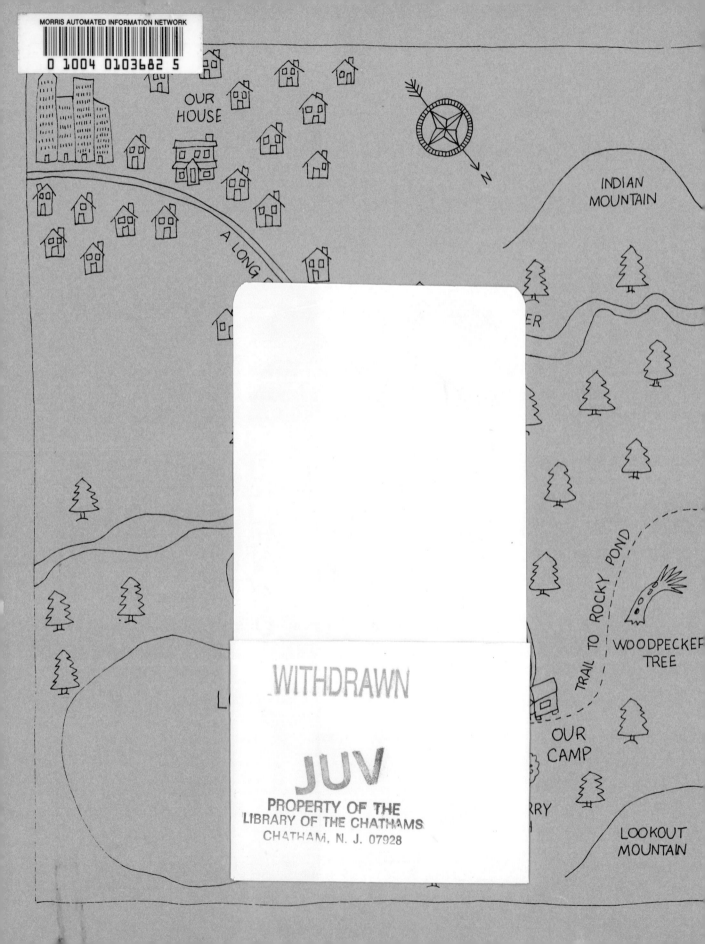